Time Stopped
on
Christmas Eve

C.E. KRAFT

Illustrated by April Jory Martin

ISBN 978-1-0980-5841-8 (paperback)
ISBN 978-1-0980-5842-5 (digital)

Christian Faith Publishing, Inc.
832 Park Avenue
Meadville, PA 16335
www.christianfaithpublishing.com

Printed in the United States of America

For my sister Claire,
Thanks for pointing out the North Pole
in our Christmas tree.

Contents

Chapter 1

Christmas Eve

It was very rare for Claire to make a joke or be anything less than serious. After all, she was a good daughter, a caring big sister, and a very responsible student.

7

Her mother was a busy seamstress who ran her business from home. For years, Mother had sewn dresses, costumes, and hems for her daughters. Now she mostly sewed for the many families in their community. Claire worried that her mother was always so busy; so she tried her best to be a big help at home.

Claire had three younger sisters to care for while Mother works hard in the tiny room on the back of their row home. It is in the front room of their small home that this story began.

Five years ago, their father died in a horrible accident that took him away from his family forever. Claire tried hard to remember all of the memories of her father at Christmas time. It was his favorite time of year. She would tell her sisters the stories of their father dressed like Santa and bringing toys to the orphanage that he carved himself in his wood shed. She would hold up the dolls that he made on the nights that each of them were born. He told Claire it would be their very first birthday gift.

He was a generous man and had a great love for seeing the faces of children light up when they received a special toy he created with his own hands. Blocks, tops, puzzles, trains, wagons; how wonderful each of their Christmases were because of his gift for creating marvelous toys.

This would be their fifth Christmas without Father. Claire missed him more than ever. She made up in her mind that on this particular Christmas she would make it a special point to sit by the Christmas tree. It was decorated with the handmade ornaments her father made out of their former Christmas trees. She would share in great detail about her joyful father to her sisters. She would not let him be forgotten. There would be plenty of time for sharing this Christmas Eve as Mom was busy finishing last minute touches on the fancy Christmas outfits her customers needed mended for tomorrow.

Claire and her sisters cleaned up after dinner and gathered around the tree. It was a small tree compared to the ones Father used to bring home, but it was still taller than Mary, who was the tallest of all her sisters.

Each girl sat facing the tree with their legs crisscrossed in front of them. As Claire began, she pointed to the first ornament, a painted wooden heart with her parents' initials carved in calligraphy on the front.

"This is the first ornament Father ever made. He gave it to Mother to celebrate their first Christmas together. He loved Mother very much and would hang lots of mistletoe around the house so that he could sneak kisses from her."

The second ornament was a wooden block with the letter *C* carved on it.

"This is the ornament Dad made for my first Christmas."

She pointed to the other wooden blocks that had the first letter of all their names on them. The girls ran their fingers over the smoothly sanded and painted blocks just to feel the places their Father had once held. With one touch a fresh memory of their father's happy face would fill their minds; except for Claire's youngest sister who was much too young to remember her father. This made Claire very sad.

There was a painted red sleigh on the Christmas tree that Father had also carved with great detail. It must have taken him a long time. It had two rows of seats inside.

The sleigh blades were painted gold. Holly and berries were carefully painted on the sides of the sled. Claire took a deep breath when she began to explain the meaning of the red sleigh her father created the last Christmas he spent with them.

"This red sleigh is probably the saddest ornament of all because it was Father's last. He told me that he had hoped to one day build a life-sized sleigh just like this to hold as many gifts as he could carve in one year. He would ride this sleigh to the orphanage and give every child he could reach a toy for Christmas."

A tear rolled over her eyelashes and onto the sled.

After Claire wiped her eyes, she watched a few of the branches on the tree sway. All of the girls stood to their feet and stared at the moving branches. Claire thought for a moment. *Had they cut down a tree with a critter living inside?*

"What's that sound?" said the smallest girl, Nicolette. They all took a step closer and put their ear to the tree. Claire could not hear anything, but she was sure she saw the tree branches moving again.

"Let's see what is causing all of this commotion," said Mary.

The four girls laid on their backs and slid their bodies under the tree until their heads nearly hit the stand. They were able to look straight up inside their Christmas tree to the top of the trunk. It was a beautiful view of all of the lights and ornaments. The sparkle and glitter made their eyes wide with delight.

Their eyes slowly moved up toward the top of the tree until they found the branches that were moving. Every girl was speechless.

Every mouth hung wide open. Everybody froze in shock.

Impossible, Claire thought. What she saw was unbelievable to this very serious kind of girl. There were tiny people walking on those branches. They were dressed in brightly colored velvet and seemed to be singing a jolly tune as they walked in a parade toward the center of the tree.

"Do you see what I see?" whispered Chrissy. "Those are not creatures I've ever seen before."

Chapter 2

A Little Surprise

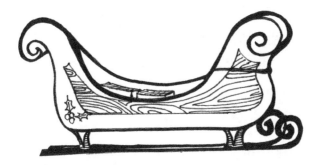

Claire rubbed her eyes. Surely she was imagining such curious things, but there was no change in her vision. These little people continued marching and singing toward the center of the tree and with them they were pulling wagons and pushing carts of what they could not see.

Who were they and where were they going?

"Hello?" called Nicolette in her small voice. "My name is Nicolette, what is your name?"

The little people did not seem to notice that the youngest girl was speaking to them.

"Hello? Can you hear us?" shouted Mary.

But it wasn't until Chrissy sneezed that the last of the little people in the parade noticed them. He was startled to a halt and tipped the wheel barrel over. Silver, sparkling dust drifted down and fell on the girls until each of them was sneezing uncontrollably.

With every sneeze the girls let out, they shrunk in size until they opened their eyes and found that they were in a place that did not seem familiar to any of them. The carpet was red felt and it appeared they were in a giant forest.

"Where are we?" asked Claire in a very serious tone. Her hands moved quickly to hold her throat as the words that came out of her mouth sounded funny.

Curious to hear her own voice, Mary said, "Wherever it is, it's beautiful. I've never seen so many bright lights before."

Mary giggled at the sound of her own voice while Chrissy inspected their surroundings more closely.

"There is something familiar about this place. Have we been here in a dream?" asked Chrissy curiously.

Nicolette grabbed on to Claire's nightgown and put her thumb in her mouth.

Claire patted the top of her youngest sister's hair, "It'll be alright, Nicolette. We'll find our way back home again."

"Um, sisters? I think we are home!" said Mary as she pointed out familiar objects around her. "Don't you recognize this carpet? It's our tree skirt! And look here…this is the biggest tree trunk I've ever seen but not one I've *never* seen."

Mary rubbed her tiny hand on the rough tree trunk.

"This is our Christmas tree. We are looking at it from a different point of view." Mary squinted her eyes. "We are looking at it from a much *smaller* point of view. *We* are *much smaller!*"

The girls huddled together. They were worried. Chrissy was the first to step away. "Maybe that silvery dust made us shrink."

Claire felt her arms, her stomach, and her legs. She felt alright. "How do you feel sisters?"

All of the girls looked each other over. They felt fine. As a matter of fact, they haven't felt so wonderful in a long time! They continued to check themselves over. Their bellies were not hungry. Their eyes were not tired. Their ears, oh, their ears were different. They were pointy!

"We're elves!" Claire exclaimed.

Nicolette and Chrissy felt their ears and giggled. Mary and Claire stared at each other for some time until Mary once again broke the silence, "Those little people in our tree must be elves!"

"I've always wanted to be an elf," said Chrissy, "I *am* small for my age. It would be the perfect job for me."

The other girls looked at Chrissy and then continued to marvel at the sights and scents around them. It seemed their noses were more sensitive from when they were normal girls. They could actually smell the fabric under their feet and the pine from the tree was so strong that it nearly burned their noses.

"We have to find those elves and see if they can make us normal size again before Mom finds us missing," Claire said with a frown.

"It's a long way up to the top of the tree," Mary complained, "I'm not good at climbing trees at my normal height. How will I ever make it to the top if I am only five inches tall?"

"It's our only hope. We have to try," Claire explained. But in her throat was a knot that she knew she could not untie or it was sure to let loose a river of sobs. She was very worried about her mother finding them missing. It would surely cause her much pain and worry.

Claire took a deep breath and said, "Let's start climbing. Nicolette, go in front of me so I can give you a boost."

As the girls made their way to the tree trunk, the red sleigh ornament Claire had just explained to her sisters appeared before them. It was lowered down by four of the elves they had seen marching. The elf that heard them was there and he was the first one to speak in a funny voice:

"I'm so sorry for dropping our shrinking powder on you. I heard the strangest sound and it startled me. The wheel barrel just slipped. If you climb into the sleigh, we can take you to see our boss and he'll be able to help you turn back to your normal size."

What else could the girls do? Their only hope was to find this elf boss and get help before Mom notices they are missing. Claire carried Nicolette into the front seat of the sleigh while Mary and Chrissy sat in the back. At once the biggest elf said, "Sit tight." And with a jolt, the sleigh began to lift off the ground and up the tree.

The girls thought the tree looked beautiful before when they were normal size, but it looked even more beautiful now. As the sled ascended higher and higher through the tree branches, they passed the beautiful bright lights, shiny tinsel, giant candy canes, and all of the ornaments their father had made.

It was like seeing his ornaments for the very first time because now the ornaments were bigger than the girls. The ornaments hung from branches like tall statues. The girls could see all of the details their human eyes missed; from the intricate carvings, to the very brush stroke of paint Father applied. Everything looked so new to them, including the little men that were lifting the sled with ease toward the top of the tree.

Chapter 3

The Doorway

They stopped the sled at the block ornament that Father made for Claire. The
block ornament sat on a branch rather than
hanging freely from its string. The little men

helped the girls get out of the sleigh and walked them toward Claire's block.

"You're going to love this," said the tallest elf.

The tall elf knocked on the front of the block and right before their eyes, the side of the block opened like a door. Just through the door was a land that was pure white.

The four little elves walked through the door as they spoke to one another. "We're behind on our work for the day now. I hope we didn't miss the snowball cookies. Pudgy makes the best cookies."

The girls followed them through the open doorway and immediately recognized the whiteness. It was snow! This snow was unique because it felt warm rather than cold, like warm powder beneath their feet. Claire wondered if it could be made into a snowball and as soon as she finished that thought, a snowball went flying past her face and smacked the tallest elf right in the back of the head.

Chrissy bent down and gathered some of this peculiar snow into her hands and formed it into a snowball.

"It feels just like snow only it's not cold. We don't need gloves!"

The girls giggled and laughed as they formed snowballs and tossed them at each other. They were lost in their playfulness until Claire remembered with all seriousness that her mother would be finished working soon and would find them gone.

"Girls, we must find help and get home again quickly."

The girls brushed the warm dust from their clothes and ran to catch up with the little elves that ironically didn't seem so little anymore. A few of them were actually taller than Mary.

As they ran, they began to notice how unique this place was. The trees were all decorated for Christmas, even in the forest they seemed to be in now. Every tree was lit up with lovely colored lights and ornaments so shiny they could see their reflection as clearly as in a mirror. They stopped to admire the differences in their appearance. Their skin was brighter, their eyes were wider, their hair was smoother, and their ears were pointed. Ha! More laughter erupted as they admired themselves in the mirror-like ornaments.

An elf wearing a long sparkly white robe, beaded with jewels came toward the girls with a huge grin on his face.

"Young ladies, it is so good to meet you after all we have heard about you. Would you please follow me?"

Claire and Mary exchanged looks. They were both thinking it odd that this elf who seemed to be more important than the others would know much about them. They were only in this strange but amazing place for a few minutes. How much could the other elves have shared with him? Still, they knew that he would be able to help them.

Claire stepped forward, "Are you the Elf Boss around here that will be able to help us get back to our mother?"

"No, no, child. I am Tucker, head err...elf, but not the Boss." Tucker smiled wide, like he knew an inside joke. "I make sure all of the..." he paused and then chuckled, "*elves* are staying on task around here. But it seems that one of our workers was startled by you four young ladies, and shrunk you down to our size. We apologize for that and will fix it as soon as our Boss is available. This is a very busy time for him. For now, would you girls like to sample some cookies and milkshakes? They are sure to be the best tasting treats you will ever try."

"We don't have much time," Claire explained, "Our mother will notice us gone in a little while and be very worried."

"Oh, no need to worry about that Claire. In this place, time doesn't exist. It may seem like you're here for hours, but it will only be a few minutes where you come from."

"Where is this place?" Chrissy asked, "Where are we?"

"So many worries for little girls…let's get you something to eat, Chrissy."

"Can I ask just one more question?" Claire spoke cautiously, "Why were your elves in our Christmas tree and how do you know our names?"

"So many questions dear girls...they will all be answered soon. Follow me to the bakery."

This head elf seemed very friendly, very nice. His long white pointed beard made him seem very wise and safe. The girls were no longer concerned about getting home before Mother notices them missing.

For some reason, they seemed carefree in their hearts. It was only their minds that thought these thoughts, but worry never reached their bellies. As a matter of fact, the girls were content in that deep place of their hearts. They were safe when they listened to this part of themselves, they did not need to worry about a thing. They were happy.

Of all the sisters, Claire noticed this joy the most. She is the oldest sister with the most responsibilities. It is rare that she can be worry-free. It is unusual for her to let someone else care for her and her sisters. But here she was walking toward a small village, with the iciest-looking streets she's ever seen. There were crystal streams that seemed to have steam coming from them. She was sure that if she dipped her toes in the stream the water would be warm like bath water.

The buildings were small on the outside, like pictures artists have drawn of the North Pole. However these buildings seemed more like gingerbread houses with candy cane trim, frosted roofs, and gumdrop mailboxes. The gates were made from pretzel logs and the scent of cinnamon was in the air. It was not just the bakery that carried this scent as all of the buildings were made from this gingerbread.

Chapter 4

A Winter Wonderland

I f her father could have seen this place, he
would be in awe. This is just the kind of
place he would have loved.

They stepped inside the bakery, which
to their surprise was much larger inside than
what the outside appeared to be. The glass
counters stretched and curved around the

entire bakeshop. In front of the big glass windows were small café-sized tables with candy cane-striped legs and painted red seats. But when Mary ran her hands over the seat, she could feel that they were hand-carved and painted to look like real candy canes.

Nicolette didn't pay attention to the details of her surroundings because the scents coming from the large glass counter distracted her too much. Her little fingers were pressed against the glass as she stretched on her tiptoes to see what goodies were there for her to choose.

Before anyone could speak, the worried thoughts in Claire's head caused her to blurt out, "How will we pay for such delicious treats, sisters?"

Tucker put his arm around her shoulders and in the kindest voice spoke, "Dear Claire, we don't use money here. You'll find this place is very different. You can have anything here, it is freely given. Please, choose what you would like and our baker will get it for you."

"Can we get pizza?" Chrissy asked.

Tucker and the baker chuckled. "Pizza is made in the pizza shop. You will have to walk a little further down the lane for that."

Claire noticed that Tucker and the head baker exchanged a meaningful look between each other. She was sure it was harmless when she listened to that inner part of herself; but she couldn't help but think suspiciously in her mind. It was as if the two older elves expected Chrissy to ask about pizza.

Each of the girls glanced up and down the glass counters, searching for the baked good that stole their attention. Pink frosting, peppermint glaze, milk chocolate, dark chocolate, white chocolate, nuts, no nuts, fruit-filled, custard-filled…there were too many choices. Finally they all made a choice and sat down at the cozy tables with a pastry as wide as their plates.

There was something familiar about the chairs and tables to all of the girls. Claire was the first to notice they were as comfortable as the chairs in their kitchen at home.

They learned the bakers name was Pudgy. Though they know that name means something mean where they are from, it seemed to be a great honor here. He spoke his name with such pride.

Pudgy gave each of the girls a Chocolate Mint Milkshake. It was frothy and delicious. It went perfectly with the pastries and cookies they had chosen to snack on. They were not hungry to begin with but they thought that these giant desserts would make them feel full quickly.

To their surprise, they could have kept eating and eating and would have never become full. It was as if they had a bottom-less pit in their stomach. On the other hand, shouldn't they at least start to feel sick from eating all of these desserts until their heart is content? But they didn't. They were healthy and as happy ever.

When they had finished their treats, they thanked Pudgy and headed toward the door. This time, Mary noticed the meaningful stares exchanged between Pudgy and Tucker.

"Claire, do you think there is something secret about this place? I feel as though these elves know us, but we don't know them. Yet, I don't feel afraid."

"I have noticed the same thing, Mary. We will just have to wait until we meet their boss. In the meantime, don't let our younger sisters know that we're being cautious, I haven't seen them so happy in a long time."

"I haven't felt so happy myself in a long time," whispered Mary. "There is something about this place. I would miss Mother, but I don't ever want to leave."

The girls wrapped an arm around each other as they stepped back out onto the shining glass streets.

This time there was something new. There was beautiful music in the air. It was like nothing they ever heard before. It was the sound of thousands of voices singing many different melodies, but all blending into one lovely song.

"That music is wonderful. Is there a concert somewhere?" Chrissy asked.

"There is one continuous concert here, dear ones. Strange that you did not notice it earlier," Tucker said like it was a question.

"Oh, how I wish I could go to this concert," Chrissy exclaimed, "It is probably the loveliest concert in the world."

Tucker chuckled, "That it is, Chrissy. That it is. Maybe my boss will let you join the concert this day."

Chrissy's eyes glistened and she began to skip to her own strand of melody that would also blend lovely with the music they all heard.

Up over a hill, they saw in front of them a mansion or maybe even a castle. This must be the place where the elf boss dwells. The road continued to wind up and down small hills, more Christmas trees on either side of the road. The girls kept their eyes roaming continually at all of the unique ornaments and lights around them. When they got closer to the castle, they saw even more lights and decorations.

This is the North Pole and the boss is Santa, Nicolette thought.

"Are we visiting Santa?" she asked out loud.

"No, young Nicolette. This is not the North Pole. It is much more special than that," Tucker laughed heartier than he had earlier.

Mary scratched her head. "So your boss isn't Santa? Who is he?"

"We are almost there," Tucker pointed out. "You will find out soon enough. I see you've brought impatience with you from home." He laughed just once more.

Chapter 5

The Castle

Large gates made from gum drops, pretzel rods, candy canes, sprinkles, and peppermints, opened up wide just in time for all of them to pass through.

The girls were getting excited now. Maybe they were excited to see what was inside of this very large castle, or maybe they were excited that they would be seeing their mother soon, which they could not tell, but their feet carried them forward even more quickly than before.

Tucker stepped up to the door and nodded his head. The door opened up by itself and what the girls saw just inside the door astounded them. Once again, the castle looked smaller on the outside then it did on the inside.

Once they stepped through the door themselves, it looked as if they could fit the entire village inside this very large room they came upon. The colors inside this place were so vibrant. There were giant sprockets and wheels turning conveyor belts that made enormous machines run.

Tucker said this wasn't the North Pole, but it sure did look like Santa's workshop. There were dolls, wagons, toy trains, and cars. There were baseball bats, footballs, doll houses, scooters, all lined up and painted different colors.

There was something very familiar about the faces on the dolls. At once Claire was shocked. To her left sat a doll on a shelf that looked exactly like Chrissy. On her right sat a stuffed dog that looked exactly like their dog Henry at home.

"What is going on here?" Claire asked firmly. "Why do these toys look just like my family?"

"Don't be alarmed, Claire. Your family is very special to the boss and he uses your faces as his inspiration for making these marvelous toys." He placed his hand under Claire's chin and tilted her face so she could read his eyes.

At once she relaxed and smiled. "Soon, my child…soon you will understand."

The girls ran up and down long rows as long as football fields filled with all sorts of toys. Each toy was unique; each toy made with such detail and love. There was something familiar about them all.

When they had come to the back of this room, there was another door with frosted glass that read, *Office*.

Tucker knocked on the door twice and a new voice answered, "Please, come in."

The door opened wide and this time the room looked like a normal-sized room. It was definitely an office with rows of file cabinets and books along two of the four walls.

The person who welcomed them stood with his back toward the girls, bent down over his desk writing with a long feather pen.

This man was different. He was not small and did not have pointed ears. He was not an elf, but a human man. Tucker said he wasn't Santa Claus, but it sure did seem like this was the North Pole. This Santa Claus was thinner than expected, but clearly in charge of the small people with funny voices that were dressed like elves.

"I'm so excited you girls are here. Please make yourselves at home," the man with the nice voice said as he wrote so quickly his hand was a blur.

The girls all took a seat on a bench on the north facing wall. Tucker closed the door behind him and left the room. Now Claire was nervous. They did not know this man and they were now alone in the room with him.

The man chuckled, "My, my, Claire. How you've become quite responsible. You are a big help to your mother and I'm very thankful for that. But I assure you, you have nothing to fear here."

With that, the man stood tall and turned to face the girls with a big grin. He was the most handsome man they had ever seen. He was strong, but gentle. He was jovial and good-natured. He was…

"Daddy!"

All four girls jumped to their feet and ran to the man who was now bent down on one knee with his arms wide open for the girls to jump in. One by one, with Nicolette being the most hesitant this time, they jumped into their father's arms.

"Let me take a look at you all. My, how you have grown so beautiful, just like your mother."

Their father kissed each of them on the forehead and squeezed all four of them over and over again. It was the sweetest reunion they could ever ask for.

They spent some time sitting on their dad's lap, sharing the memories they had of his time at home and telling him of the things he has missed in the past few years, like Claire having lost all of her baby teeth, Mary breaking her finger last summer playing baseball with the boys in the neighborhood, and Nicolette singing, "Away in the Manger" at the church Christmas pageant.

Chapter 6

Sweet Reunions

Father was so proud of his daughters and told them that he misses them very much, but the time where he lives now is very different, so that it only feels like he has been away from his family for a few hours rather than a few years.

Claire's heart swelled with this news because she was glad that at least one of them was not feeling the pain of missing the other. She could tell her dad was very happy where he lived now. It was a good thing that he missed them but could not feel the time that he lost with them. He missed them enough to show her he loved them very much, but not enough for her to see him hurting by his absence from his family.

"Come with me, girls. There are some things I'd like to show you." Father grabbed the two younger girls' hands and went back out into the toy factory.

"You know how much I enjoyed seeing your faces when I gave you toys that I made with my own hands? Do you remember how much I loved making toys to give to the orphanage?" The girls nodded with excitement. "Well you see…my job here is to do what I love. I create toys that we secretly place in the hands of unsuspecting children who have nothing for Christmas. In a way, I'm a secret Santa."

The girls laughed together while Father picked up the doll that looked like Chrissy.

"When you found my helpers in your Christmas tree, they were there to see how you girls have changed so that I can make new molds for my dolls here. Every year, my dolls change a little bit because I design them after the most beautiful girls I know…my daughters," Father beamed.

"Your elves are very funny and very nice. They didn't tell us too much about this place," Mary said.

"Oh, they are not elves, Mary. My helpers are angels. Now that you mention it, they do sort of look like angelic elves. God knows what I like. He knows that Christmas is my favorite time of year. He designed this whole village to my liking. He is so gracious even here where we are already so content and don't need anything more."

Claire rubbed her chin and looked at Father curiously. "Father, are we in heaven with you? And why do we look like your elves…err, angels?"

Father laughed. "Yes, I am sorry about that. They seemed to have dropped their angel dust on you. It shrinks them down so that they can visit you inconspicuously, though it seems they weren't as careful as they usually are. But this is one part of heaven where I mostly work. Would you like to see more of this wonderful place?"

Father walked them outside, down a jeweled pathway and into a greenhouse.

"Claire, I had this built so that we could work closely together some day."

It is important to understand that Claire had never been able to go into a greenhouse because she immediately broke out into hives and had trouble breathing.

She was severely allergic to many flowers and up until this point, could only stare at flowers and plants when she read about them in magazines or encyclopedias. This was sad indeed, for Claire loved flowers and plants.

Whenever Father brought home flowers for Mother, Claire would arrange them in their vase and rearrange them as many times as she could before the sneezing and itching got out of control. Mother would always be upset with her for allowing the allergic reaction to get so bad, but Claire could not help it. The different colors and shapes of the petals were hypnotic.

To be surrounded by so many beautiful flowers and plants would send Claire into an immediate reaction so she paused at the entry way of the greenhouse and admired its loveliness from there.

"It's alright Claire, you won't be allergic to these flowers," Father said as he escorted her further through the door.

The fragrances from the enchanting flowers overwhelmed Claire. She inhaled over and over again, waiting for the faint memory of those pesky, itchy hives to attack her neck and arms. She was still as she waited for her eyes to water or a sneeze to escape. Neither ever came.

She looked at her Dad and asked, "How is it possible?"

"How gracious is our God that your first encounter with gardening is here in heaven? He wanted you to see exactly how beautiful his creation is meant to be without getting sick. You don't realize yet, but you not only have a green thumb, you have a gift for arranging flowers in a way nobody else could see. You have a way of seeing the flowers paired off the way God had seen it from the beginning. Go ahead, play with the flowers. Touch them. It's alright."

Chapter 7

The Greenhouse

To a little girl of twelve years old, a green-house might not seem exciting. But in all her twelve years, Claire could never touch and arrange these exquisite treasures that so intrigued her. This was her dream.

She slowly approached the rows and rows of freshly cut flowers. She chose luxurious blossoms of white roses, double lisianthus in a purple-blue shade, white limonium, and yellow lilies. She arranged them together with assorted lush greens. The colors and aromas took her breath away.

She stepped back and saw that everyone around her was also marveling at what she put together so stunningly.

She noticed Mary was not as enthused as everyone else. She decided to make Mary a wreath to wear home. She chose four delphinium blossoms, two yellow roses, a stem of baby's breath, and white sheer ribbon. She got to work at once using wire and floral tape to make the most magnificent wreath for her sister to wear. She placed the wreath on Mary's head. Mary beamed from ear to ear at her delightful gift.

"Thank you," Mary said looking down at her feet.

"Well done, Claire. You're a natural floral designer," beamed her proud father.

All of the girls were very excited to see more. Chrissy was most eager to find out where the music was coming from.

Father seemed to know this, because he looked right at Chrissy and said, "Don't worry, Chrissy. I'm most excited to show you the very large choir. We all know how fond of music you and Nicolette are. Perhaps I'll get to see little Nicolette sing for myself."

Father showed them around the rest of his village and many others while they walked down the streets of pure gold. They even got to sample some pizza from the pizza shop Father said he placed there for Chrissy.

Each village was unique for the person who ran it. Each village was covered in a different landscape. There was one village that was sand and ocean, and another that was meadows. There was one with mountains, and others prairies with streams running through them. There were Tudor-style homes nestled in forests, and log cabin-style homes near lakes.

Mary's favorite was the one that looked like the most expensive city in the world. It had tall crystal buildings, with many gold streets running up and down in rows. There were many angels hustling and bustling on the clean sidewalks. There were glass trains that ran on an energy that did not expend any pollution.

Father stopped near this city and spoke to Mary, "When you were just three years old, Mother and I took you to New York City. Oh, how you got excited by all that was going on in that busy place. You seemed right at home in all the hubbub. There is a building here that I know you would like to see."

Mary smiled at her dad. It was curious to her that she felt like they had never spent five years apart.

She held her father's hand tightly as they walked down the busy streets. Chrissy and Nicolette swung their arms while holding hands with Tucker and Pudgy, while Claire lagged behind, still thinking about her mother since Father mentioned her again.

They stopped in front of a library. They walked up at least fifty steps to the rotating library doors yet they all felt they could walk up fifty more and never get tired.

Father stopped just outside the doors and looked at Mary, "We can only take a peek inside. We can't look through the books because there are books here that have not been written yet on earth and we can't give away any secrets. I can tell you that there are a few books in this library that will be written by you someday, Mary. You are a creative, bright girl and your books entertained me the most. Be patient and persistent. Keep practicing your writing."

Father smiled proudly and hugged Mary tight. "Would you like to take a peek into the most extravagant library in existence?"

"Yes!" shouted all of the girls. With that, they stepped inside and Mary's eyes widened with astonishment.

The size of the library was deceiving from the outside. From inside, the library was cylindrical and extended at least twenty stories high from the level they entered.

They walked to the railing in front of them and looked down to at least twenty more stories below. If they were allowed to explore any further, they would follow the ramps up in a spiral around the book shelves in either direction with one leading upward and the other leading downward to the levels above and below.

It was the most unique building they have ever seen. There was a large circular stained glass window on the ceiling. It looked small from where they stood but their vision was exceptional. They could see that it was not stained glass like one would see in churches on earth, but a mosaic of brightly colored jewels. It was the most beautiful mosaic of Mary, Joseph, and baby Jesus in the stable, surrounded by animals. It read, "The Greatest Story Ever Told." The music that was in the air rang loud and clear from this piece of glass art.

Beautiful, Claire thought as they left the city.

Chapter 8

The Music Hall

It was no wonder that people here did not miss what they had left on earth. They had the best of everything right here. Each village they had passed on their way was designed precisely for the inhabitant it was made for. The joyous music that was so captivating in

Father's village was also so beautiful in all the others.

They finally reached the main city. You could tell it was just that because it had blended the best features of all the other villages into one stunning city. They had walked for what seemed hours in human time, but felt like just moments in heaven. Though they walked for miles and miles, no one was tired. Not one was weary. Nobody needed to sit or rest.

They approached a building that was majestically jeweled in emeralds, rubies, and diamonds carved in the shapes of music notes and clefs. There were piano keys running across the roof made from pearl and onyx. The building itself was a crystal sculpture but the melody proceeding from beyond its walls was enchanting.

Chrissy and Nicolette were drawn inside, mesmerized by the music. They were greeted by an usher who was a giant. His head nearly touched the ceiling which had to be seventeen feet high. Though his features were large, they were beautiful and angelic. Claire assumed that this giant man must also be a type of angel.

"Welcome to the music hall," said the giant. My name is Opus, aren't you early?"

"Hello, Opus," Father spoke, "They are only visiting this day."

"Oh, I see. So they have not met the Most High?"

"No, not yet and not until they finish all he has called them to do on earth. I'm most honored that he allowed them to come this far in the kingdom."

Opus looked over each girl with a large grin. "Yes, it is a great honor indeed. I wonder how much they'll remember when they get back home."

Claire was confused. She did not want to forget one moment she had spent with her father in this most amazing of all places.

She did not want to leave. However, somewhere in her mind, though she had not thought of it in a long while, she did miss her mom and knew how difficult it would be for Mother if she and her sisters never went back. But how could she forget such a wonderful day?

"Father, I could never forget this time with you. It is the most wonderful gift my sisters and I could ever receive."

Father squeezed Claire's shoulders, "Now, now, you will never forget and if you do I should remind you when I see you next." Claire smiled. Her father always knew how to comfort her.

Chrissy and Nicolette were already through the doors leading to the auditorium. Just like all the other buildings they visited, this one somehow magically grew to be at least a hundred times larger than what it had appeared on the outside.

There was a large choir on the stage. It was so big that you could not see where either side ended as it curved behind the stage as far as the eye could see. Each section of the choir must have had thousands of singers conducted by its own director.

The stage moved slowly in rotation with all the singers and directors singing their own melody but somehow blending to make one beautiful song. It was a song the girls had never heard with their human ears before.

Nicolette already took her place in the front row of one of the sections singing as though she knew her part well and had rehearsed it all her life.

Chrissy stood before one of the sections and directed the voices in a way she did not know her abilities would allow for a girl of just eight years. She looked to her left and right to see the other directors doing exactly what she did without needing to coordinate.

Both of the youngest sisters felt very much at home and as if they could be part of this giant choir and never grow tired.

Eventually, Father called the girls to come down from the choir and join their other two sisters. His large arms wrapped around all four of them and his face was buried in their hair. It was time for the children to go home. The girls held their arms tightly around Father's waist while standing on the steps of the music hall. They were unable to weep because there is no sorrow or weeping in heaven.

Somehow, they understood that this was the best Christmas gift they could ask for, seeing their Father once more. They prayed that his face, his smell, his voice would linger with them for all time.

"I love you, my little angels," Father whispered over their heads.

And it was like this, huddled together with their eyes squeezed tightly closed that they came to find themselves under the Christmas tree, which was now back to normal size.

Chapter 9

Christmas Miracles

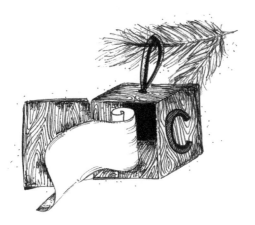

"Girls, what on *earth* are you doing under the Christmas tree?" They heard their mother's voice say.

What on earth? That is when they realized they were indeed on earth once again, where they needed to be for their mother and to live happily until they see their father and heavenly Father again.

Claire was the first to stand to her feet. The first thing she did was grab her ears. She was disappointed to find that they were no longer pointed. Come to think of it, the other angels they met did not have pointed ears. It was only the ones that helped her father.

Maybe it was just a silly dream. Her sisters were still lolling under the tree sleepily.

She ran to her mother and wrapped her arms around her waist.

"Mother, Merry Christmas!"

"Merry Christmas, Claire," Mother said. "Did you arrange the beautiful flowers that were left on the front porch?"

"No, I didn't, Mother. I would never. I know it upsets you when they make me so sick."

"I'm glad to hear that. It is the most beautiful arrangement. I thought for sure it was something you created." She kissed her daughter's forehead, "You're the only one I know who can pair together the most breath-taking arrangements."

Claire smiled.

Mother gathered up the rest of Claire's sisters and helped them to their beds. All of the girls were rubbing their eyes, but she did notice little Nicolette grabbing her ears.

Could it have been real? Did Claire and her sisters really visit their father in heaven?

No way, thought Claire. *Impossible.*

Or could it be? Claire immediately ran to the Christmas tree to find the block ornament her father made for her. She pulled it from the branch it rested on and began turning it in her hand, trying to find the hinged side that the little elves, um, angels, had opened to lead them into her father's village.

Over and over again, she turned the block until finally, the block opened, revealing a small roll of paper inside. Carefully she pulled out the paper and then held her eye up to the opening in the block.

It was dark inside, no sign of warm snow. She held her ear to it, but there was no sound of the beautiful music.

It was just a dream.

Claire unrolled the piece of paper, and sat in the big chair by the window to read it. It was her father's handwriting and it said:

How Gracious is our God!
May you never forget.
I love you, my Angel!
Daddy

Henry jumped on the big chair and licked Claire's hand that held the note.

"It was just a dream, Henry. How silly I was to believe it was real even for a second," she whispered to her dog as she stroked behind his ears.

She heard Mother on the front porch. She heard glass break and her mother's voice, "Oh dear."

She ran to the front door and saw her mother crouched over flowers and a broken vase.

"Let me help you, Mother."

"No, no. I don't want you to be sick for Christmas, your allergic remember?"

Something in Claire pushed her forward to the place where her mother was and she bent down to help clean up the glass.

What she did not expect was that the flowers were the very same that she had arranged in the greenhouse in her dream.

She picked up a white rose and put it to her nose.

"What on earth are you doing, Claire? You'll break out into hives!" Mother pleaded.

"Don't worry Mother; I could do it in heaven. I'm not allergic anymore."

And it was the truth. She gathered all the flowers in her arms while Mother picked up the rest of the glass.

She headed back inside, but not until she realized the wreath she made for Mary's head was hanging on their front door.

Claire smiled to herself and arranged the flowers over and over again until they were as perfect as they were in heaven. Mother's face showed all amazement and joy. It was a miracle!

Claire never saw another hive again. It was a Christmas gift from her heavenly Father.

The rest of her sisters were never the same either. Mary began writing stories immediately and by some coincidence, Mother had given her special paper and pencils on Christmas morning.

Chrissy and Nicolette also received a special surprise on Christmas morning. It was a toy piano with a tag on it, "From Secret Santa." It had special carvings that were very familiar.

Mother eyed the piano suspiciously and ran her hand over the carvings with tears in her eyes.

Nicolette's singing improved every year while Chrissy began composing music immediately upon receiving that toy piano.

Somehow, even Mother seemed less sad after that Christmas Eve when she received the flowers that came from heaven.

It would be a long time before the girls could ever be with their daddy again and though that would make most people sad, it made the girls exceptionally happy.

The moment they stepped into heaven, they knew their heavenly Father, and from that moment on, they would never be father-less again.

They remembered in heaven time passed differently and it would only feel like a few moments passed to their father on the next time they meet.

So they would live that same way, moment by moment, completing the work their heavenly Father gifted them to do and getting to know him better until they meet him face to face.

About the Author

Christine E. Kraft holds a master's degree in education, is an elementary teacher and reading specialist. She loves anything purple or that walks on four legs, but not things that are purple *and* walks on four legs (that is just weird). She writes from her home in Pennsylvania, where she lives with her husband and their three children. When not reading or writing, she enjoys spending time with her musical family.

Visit the author's website at www.cekraft.com